PEOPLE DON'T

words by LISA WHEELER

ATHENEUM BOOKS FOR YOUNG READERS

BITE PEOPLE

art by MOLLY IDLE

NEW YORK LONDON TORONTO SYDNEY NEW DELHI

It's good to bite a carrot.
It's good to bite a steak.
It's BAD to bite your sister!
She's not a piece of cake.

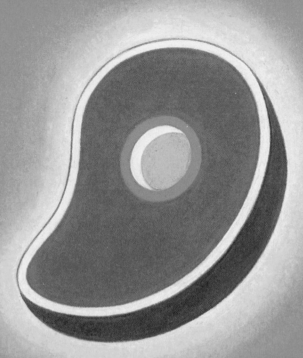

It's good to bite a biscuit.
It's good to bite a plum.
It's BAD to bite your brother.
He's not a piece of gum.

'Cause . . .

People don't bite people.
It's nasty and it's rude!
A friend will never
bite a friend.
BITING IS FOR FOOD!

A dog may bite.
A horse may bite.
They're animals,
you see.

But we can choose to use our words.

We're people, you and me.

A friend might shout
  and take your toy
or even pull your hair.
But here's a tip: Just close your lip!
You're not a grizzly bear!

Oh . . .

People don't bite people.
No matter what their mood.
A friend will never bite a friend.

BITING
IS
FOR
FOOD!

Some
people
bite
their
bottom
lips.

Some
chew
their
ponytails.

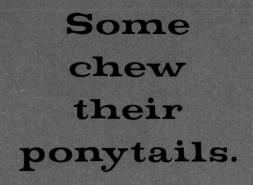

Some people tell you, "Bite your tongue!"

Some people bite their nails.

It's gross to bite the skin you're in . . .

but worse to bite another.

DO NOT attack!
   Go get a snack!
It's bad to bite
   your mother!

Yes . . .

People don't bite people.
It's no fun being chewed!
A friend will never bite a friend.

BITING
IS
FOR
FOOD!

A great white shark bites everything.

A gray
wolf
bites a
bone.

But what
YOU
chew is up to
YOU!

Your
chompers
are
your
own.

You're NOT a shark!
  You're NOT a wolf!
But sometimes you get mad.
LET IT GO! Just say no!
It's bad to bite your dad!

Say it with me!

People don't bite people.
You're not a zombie, dude!
A friend will never bite a friend.

BITING
IS
FOR
FOOD!

Puppies bite

and babies bite.

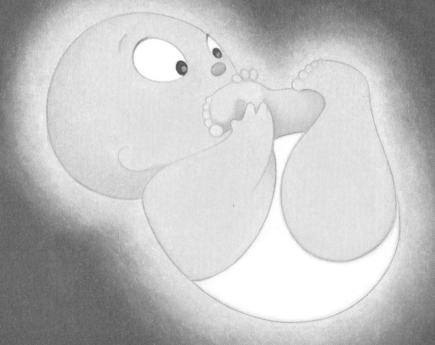

**They're much too young to know.
But you grow bigger every day
and know where teeth should go.**

You're on a roll, so take control.
You'll handle it with style.
Your teeth are meant for eating FOOD
and shining up your smile!

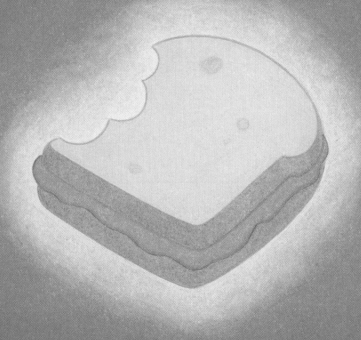

Please . . .

People don't bite people!
It really isn't right.

But if their head is gingerbread . . .

go on and take a bite!

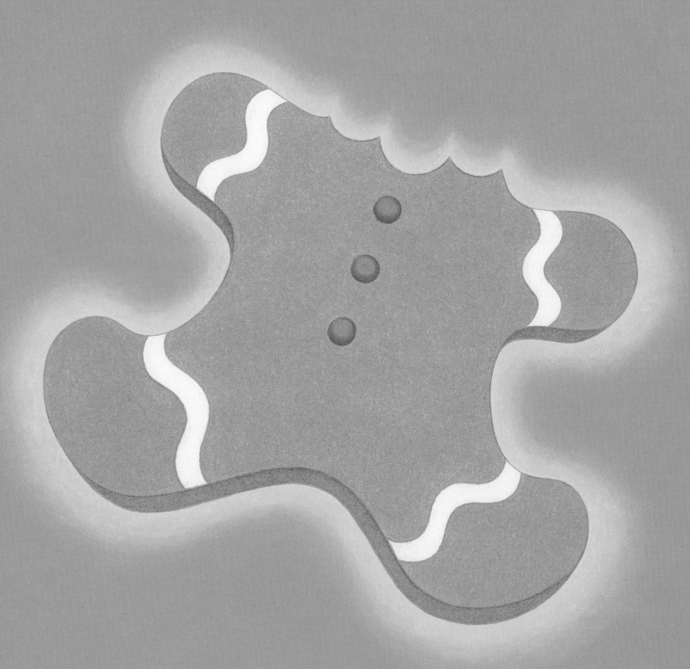

To the good folks
at Dr. Charles Sattler's dentist office
in Trenton, Michigan.
Thanks for shining up my smile!

A special thank-you to the cast
of *TWD* for the inspiration.

—L.W.

For the pearly whites and biting wits
of the Schaar Sisters
—M. I.

atheneum

ATHENEUM BOOKS FOR YOUNG READERS • An imprint of Simon & Schuster Children's Publishing Division • 1230 Avenue of the Americas, New York, New York 10020 • Text copyright © 2018 by Lisa Wheeler • Illustrations copyright © 2018 by Molly Idle • All rights reserved, including the right of reproduction in whole or in part in any form. • ATHENEUM BOOKS FOR YOUNG READERS is a registered trademark of Simon & Schuster, Inc. Atheneum logo is a trademark of Simon & Schuster, Inc. • For information about special discounts for bulk purchases, please contact Simon & Schuster Special Sales at 1–866–506–1949 or business@simonandschuster.com. • The Simon & Schuster Speakers Bureau can bring authors to your live event. For more information or to book an event, contact the Simon & Schuster Speakers Bureau at 1–866–248–3049 or visit our website at www.simonspeakers.com. • Book design by Ann Bobco • The text for this book was set in Mister Sinatra. • The illustrations for this book were rendered with Prismacolor pencils. • Manufactured in China • 0118 SCP • First Edition • 10 9 8 7 6 5 4 3 2 1 • Library of Congress Cataloging–in–Publication Data • Names: Wheeler, Lisa, 1963– author. | Idle, Molly Schaar, illustrator. • Title: People don't bite people / written by Lisa Wheeler ; illustrated by Molly Idle. • Other titles: People do not bite people • Description: First edition. | New York : Atheneum, [2018] | Summary: Illustrations and rhyming text urge children to use their teeth for biting food, not their friends or relatives. • Identifiers: LCCN 2016030003 | ISBN 9781481490825 (hardcover) | ISBN 9781481490832 (eBook) • Subjects: | CYAC: Stories in rhyme. | Behavior Fiction. | Humorous stories. • Classification: LCC PZ8.3.W5668 Peo 2018 | DDC [E]— dc23 • LC record available at https://lccn.loc.gov/2016030003